MINTY AND THE MONSTER

A SECURITY DIRECTORATE SHORT STORY

ALEXANDRIA BLAELOCK

Also by Alexandria Blaelock

SHORT STORY COLLECTIONS
The Histories of Hayward Hall
Lovelorn, Lovestruck and Love at First Sight
Common or Garden Variety Heroes
Case Files of the Wilkinson Detective Agency
Unavoidable Fates
Christmas Travesties
Five Faces of Felicia Clarke
Little Place Called Home

FICTION
That Love Nonsense
Taipan vs Brown
The Ghost and Ms Cox
Friends Like That

MS BLAELOCK'S BOOKS
Stress Free Dinner Parties
Signature Wardrobe Planning
Holistic Personal Finance
Minimally Viable Housekeeping
Planning a Life Worth Living

A SELECTION OF AVAILABLE SHORT STORIES
Alma's Grace
Fate in Your Hands
Lady of the Looking Glass
Morning Star, Evening Star, Superstar
Secret Singer
Shining Star
Ship in a Bottle
Simone Says Hands in the Air
The Day the Schedule Broke

MINTY AND THE MONSTER

A SECURITY DIRECTORATE SHORT STORY

ALEXANDRIA BLAELOCK

BlueMere Books
MELBOURNE, AUSTRALIA

For permission requests, please contact
enquiries@bluemerebooks.com.

Ordering Information:
Discounts are available on quantity purchases. For details, contact orders@bluemerebooks.com.

Minty and the Monster/Alexandria Blaelock
paperback ISBN: 978-1-922744-74-6
digital ISBN: 978-1-922744-75-3

Book Layout © BookDesignTemplates.com
Cover Art © Michael Külbe/Depositphotos

MINTY AND THE MONSTER

Apparently, the cave was magical.

At least if you believed in that kind of thing.

And newly graduated second Lieutenant Minty Hollister definitely did not believe in magic.

A Eugenics Programme success, she'd passed the Genomics Bureau post-natal testing, survived the State Academy of Cultural Regulation with a useful genetic "superpower" and graduated from the University of Civilisation.

She *knew* she was the one who made magic.

Not the traditional abracadabra kind of magic. Her genetic "superpower" was the ability to get inside people's heads to discover their dreams, the ones they didn't know they had.

And then she made it feel like they'd come true.

It was a different kind of magic entirely, even if it was just the kind that involved a fistful of glitter.

And the Cabaret Cave renovation was the magical triumph of dream infused marketing hype.

Not that all dreams were so concrete or permanent. And not that they didn't come and go according to the fortunes of each minute of every day.

Standing in the artfully reconstructed wilderness outside the main entrance, Minty tried, one-handed, to poke some loose hair back into her regulation chignon. Failing charmingly, she clutched her clipboard and prepared to enter the cave.

If anything went wrong at the inaugural Distinguished Service Awards dinner, her career would be over before it had begun.

The job of a glorified party planner was not what she'd had in mind as she'd worked her way through the University of Civilisation.

But the Authorities supposedly allocated work placements on the basis of your powers and grades, so she had to wonder. Was this her ideal calling, had she messed up big-time, or was this just one small step on the way to something more significant?

Though in some ways, the transitory nature of event planning was its own reward. Like a magic trick that surprises you for an instant, and leaves you wondering how the magician did it for a long time after.

A brief, but intense experience that seemingly changed the world forever.

And while Chef Joshua Richards was the Cave's Commandant, in charge of personnel discipline and welfare, she was now in charge of operations at this beautiful venue, so she couldn't really complain too much.

Even though she was terrified of messing it up.

They'd fenced the wide mouth of the cave in wrought iron with a beautifully large and strangely hypnotic, sinuous vine motif. The centrally located gates folded back to reveal a gentle slope down into the side of the mountain.

From this vantage point, the wide path seemed smooth, which was just as well, because the glistening limestone formations were stunningly distracting. Huge folds of warm red, ochre and brown stalactite drapery hung from the ceiling. Stalagmite columns rose from the ground, and flowstone waterfalls fell from outcroppings in the walls.

Closing her mouth, she tore her gaze from the roof and focused on the ground. Pulling a small torch from her pocket, she played the light across the ground looking for trip hazards.

Discrete lights focused on the formations along the way; garlands of flowers, an elephant, and an old man's face, among others. Not bright enough to damage them, but bright enough to cast enough light to walk down the path without faltering.

It looked good. She put the torch away, pulled a cute, glittery cat topped pen from behind her ear and ticked a box on her checklist.

So far, so good. It looked a lot like the image she'd plucked from the Deputy Director-General's mind.

And she really hoped she never had to do that again - the man's mind was a nightmare vision of possibility.

After leaving his office, she'd had to take a quick trip to the bathroom to vomit up the nastiness she'd seen.

Unfortunately, not as easy to forget, especially standing in the middle of his dream come true project.

How could someone who could dream up something as pretty as this could also dream up so much nastiness?

As she descended further, phantasms from the Deputy Director-General's head were all around her and failing someone whose superpower was to remove nastiness, an industrial-strength psy-vacuum would be the next best thing.

Only she wasn't entirely sure that either of those things actually existed.

The calming, and pleasantly earthy smell of mud rose to meet her as she descended. The drainage channels by the side of the path seemed to do their jobs and earned a tick.

The cave's interior grew cooler, but compared to the heat outside, it was comfortable. The depth should ensure it seemed comfortably warm in winter too.

She paused before the glass doors to the cave foyer, and growled as she shook herself like a dog to dissipate the Deputy Director-General's residual negative energy before entering.

The renovations had left the fundamental structure of the cave intact. They'd coated the concrete piers supporting the roof in a gritty resin mixture to resemble more natural formations, so the transition from resin to roof was almost imperceptible.

She nodded and added a tick to the list.

The earth-coloured terrazzo floor had settled nicely level and unbroken on the ground. With the top layer polished back to a fine shine, it looked as if the floor was speckled with gold dust.

And it probably was.

Another tick on the list.

Minty took a quick trip through the bathrooms, admiring the redwood cubicles, turning on all the chrome-plated taps, and flushing all the white porcelain sanitary ware. Plenty of soft paper goods and lightly citrus-scented soap in the dispensers.

She looked in the spotless mirror and tried to adjust her hair again. It was like it had a life of its own, completely independent of her.

"What do you want?" she asked it.

"What do *you* want?" her echo replied.

A lock fell loose from behind her ear.

It seemed her hair wanted to be free.

She sighed and left it where it was as she turned to survey the room one last time. It was entirely possible the luxury finishes would make a trip to the facilities a highlight of the evening. If not the highlight.

For those who didn't win, anyway.

Tick, tick, tick, and tick.

The cloakroom sported a curved reception counter in the same redwood, and across the top of it, she saw rows of wooden lockers of various sizes, each with a small numbered chrome tag hanging from the door. Minty walked through the room, giving each row a cursory glance, on guard for ugliness.

From a guest perspective, all good, another tick.

Depending on the function size and number of attendants, it would probably be a nightmarish place to work, but that wasn't her problem.

Actually, it kind of was, but she couldn't do anything about it. And none of the Senior Officers cared about the "goons" anyway.

She, on the other hand, did.

In her eyes, the fact that the Privates hadn't shown "useful" powers at the Academy of Cultural Regulation didn't make them any less human. Not to mention that someone had to take out the trash.

And as they were the steel spine of the Protection Squad, it was at least appropriate to treat them with courtesy, and address them by rank the same as Officers.

Just past the cloakroom was a board with the seating plan, beside a small white-clothed table ready to be laid out with glasses of champagne as the guests arrived.

And just past that, the main function room entrance was through an artfully constructed rockfall. It looked entirely natural, even inspecting it closely, and she wondered whether they'd blown a hole to make it.

Surely not.

Would they?

She diligently ticked another box on her checklist.

All the overhead lights shone steadily and silently; another tick.

Ten round tables danced around an open space in the middle of the room. Each had ten chairs (check), white tablecloths (check), and laid with white and silver-coloured settings for ten (check). An arrangement of yellow roses sat within a silver candelabra in the centre, one condiment set on either side (check).

She leaned over to examine the flowers at the closest table. They were fresh, unmarked, and unscented. Almost too perfect to be the real (and expensive) flowers she knew they were.

Were they "natural" or did someone have a superpower that produced perfect flowers?

She walked across the dance floor to the small raised dais on the other side. Her heels clicked smartly on the terrazzo but barely echoed in the large room.

She climbed the stairs to find the small stage was neat and clean, furnished only with a lectern and flag-covered table ready to receive the medals.

She stood behind the lectern and switched on the power. The tiny reading lamp flickered on, and as the computer powered up, the teleprompters reflected the text of the first speech back at the lectern. Hopefully already adjusted for the height of the Awards host.

Putting her clipboard down, she held the edges of the lectern in both hands and looked out over the tables and imaginary seated diners. It felt like a position of power. All those people looking expectantly up at her.

It made her uncomfortable and excited at the same time. This felt like the place where one small step at the wrong time would send your life in a different direction entirely.

Or maybe the right time.

She could almost feel a multitude of different lives spilling out from her as the seconds passed.

The symmetrically organised main floor looked good from this vantage point, so she cleared her throat and signalled the Private in charge of lighting. He obediently flicked a switch.

The room plunged momentarily into darkness, before the strings of tiny golden lights set into the walls and ceiling silently lit up like a billion stars.

Or given it was a cave, fireflies.

Or if you wanted to keep the magic theme going, like fairies.

After a moment, when the globes had adequately warmed up, and they started flickering at seemingly random intervals.

The effect was really beautiful, and for a moment, Minty was stabbed by bitter envy of the Directorate Officers who would attend the Awards Dinner that evening.

Partly because they would be guests enjoying the just rewards of their hard work, and partly because it was ever so unlikely that anyone ever from the Propaganda Bureau would ever attend an Awards dinner to receive a Distinguished Service Medal.

Let alone her.

Or get to wear a long, sparkly, swishy dress. Maybe something in a lime green.

Though technically any event she went to (ever) would be in her black dress uniform, not a long, sparkly swishy dress. Which was a shame, because no matter what anyone said, black was just not her colour.

But like every other Directorate Officer, she couldn't use her superpower on herself. Which, as far as everyone else was concerned, was probably a good thing, otherwise the world would drown in glitter.

Not that dreams came true with no obvious effort on the dreamer's part, but it would have been nice to have a clear path to follow.

Even if it was knee-deep in glitter.

Though that's probably how she'd know it was the right path anyway, because it was strewn with glitter.

Maybe it was worth keeping a lookout for glitter where she least expected it.

But in the meantime, back to the job at hand.

She scratched the back of her neck with slightly longer than regulation fingernails and ticked a bunch of boxes on her checklist.

A quick check of her watch revealed it was T minus five hours.

"Private," she said, partly to test the sound.

"Ma'am," he said as he saluted.

"You may stand down. Please put the overheads back on, and be ready to resume your duties at 17:00 hours."

"Ma'am."

He switched the lights, saluted, then turned on his heel and left the room.

"Thank you, Private."

She turned off the lectern, ticked a few more boxes, and that was the function room cleared.

Stifling the temptation to thoroughly scratch her head with both hands, she took off her cap and used the cat end of her pen to scratch the top of it, dislodging a little more hair.

She knew this jittery, itchy feeling was just apprehension, and that it would subside once the event started. In the meantime, she just had to ignore it as best she could and keep going.

Putting her cap back on, she turned towards the operational side of the cave and walked down the service corridor to the kitchens.

A few Privates had started the food preparation, and something deliciously savoury already scented the air.

The office door was open, revealing Chef at his desk, so she knocked on the door frame.

He nodded toward her and stood as she took a couple of steps into the room and saluted, dislodging a few specks of glitter onto her shoulder.

He smiled, almost imperceptibly, "at ease Lieutenant."

She relaxed slightly, "thank you Chef. Just checking the renovations meet your requirements?"

"They completed the kitchens to my specifications, and all appliances are operating satisfactorily."

She nodded and ticked off a few items on the checklist, "do you have all the staff and supplies you need?"

He glanced at his watch, "all staff have received their commissions, and are familiar with the venue. We've made a practice run, and have all the equipment we need."

She nodded again and added some ticks and notes on her checklist.

"You flew in from your previous post this morning?"

"Yes Sir."

"Have you eaten?"

"No Sir."

He stepped past her, out of this office and shouted, "Jones."

"Yes Chef!"

"The soup please."

"Yes Chef!" the Private, picked up a wire basket containing a small vacuum flask and a bowl with a bread roll in it and brought it over.

"Thank you Private," Chef said, and took the basket. He nodded and walked back to his station.

Minty was momentarily stunned by Chef's politeness, though she supposed the kitchen was an intensely intimate working space with different relational norms to the usual.

She'd read his profile, and it suggested he was not just well-respected, but well-liked too.

"Your trunk arrived yesterday, and the maid service has unpacked for you. Your dress uniform is cleaned and pressed, so you're good to go for this evening."

Which was unexpected as well as kind. She hadn't been looking forward to trying to press her uniform before the event.

"I'll show you to your quarters. You can take a break for an hour or two to rest and have a snack before the evening gets going."

And as soon as he said it, she suddenly felt tired, and a nap sounded like the best idea ever.

She drooped a little as she followed him out of the kitchen and down a warren of corridors.

While she'd memorised the floor plan, she was quickly disoriented, and was relieved to see the Directorate standard coloured navigation strips on the walls.

At least knowing the address of her rooms, she'd be able to find her way until she knew the place better.

He opened the door and walked through a small secretarial office furnished with the same redwood and chrome fixtures as the function rooms, smelling of leather and cigar smoke.

Through a solid wood door to a more spacious main office in the same style.

Her jaw dropped at the size and luxuriousness; she was very conscious of its polished perfection in contrast to her own nebulous loosey gooseiness.

Was all this just for her?

Probably not.

The décor must be more about those seeking a once in a lifetime event than her. Something imposing and awe-inspiring that would make Directorate Officers feel appropriately cared for.

But as she turned, trying to take it all in, she noticed a few small specks of gold in the terrazzo floor and was comforted.

Anyway, after a point, she'd probably wouldn't even notice the décor.

Chef put the basket on the desk, then handed her the key. "I'll leave you to rest. The guests will start arriving at 18:00, so please call past the kitchen around 17:00, so I know you're up and okay."

"Thank you Sir."

As he shut the door behind him, she threw her cap on the desk and dug her fingers into her scalp for a good hard scratch. Pins plinked to the floor as her hair unravelled, but she ignored them.

Through a door hidden in a bookshelf, she accessed a corridor containing a kitchenette on one side, and an enclosed bathroom on the other. She stopped to use the facilities, barely noticing the same high-quality fixtures as the public bathrooms at the entry.

She yawned as she went through to the last room in the suite; the bedroom. An enormous bed, crisp white bedding, and a vase of perfect, highly scented yellow roses on a chest of drawers.

Though who they thought she'd be entertaining in here was a matter to think about another day.

After travelling halfway around the world in the last thirty-six hours, she abruptly ran out of backup power and was asleep almost before her fully clothed body hit the bed.

«« • »»

Minty stood at ease in the entry foyer. To the Privates stationed here and there, she appeared calm and serene, but she was as nervous as all hell and itched all over.

Nothing to do with her immaculate uniform, or the soft citrus-scented soap she'd bathed with, just the usual pre-event jitters.

There was a rumour the Director General himself would be in attendance. It seemed unlikely, and she wasn't sure whether she hoped he would or wouldn't.

She wasn't supposed to read people without their permission, and generally wore gloves to prevent it, but sometimes a little something got through when she couldn't control her excitement. Or perhaps they couldn't conceal theirs.

What would his dreams be like?

She remembered the nastiness of his deputy's mind and swallowed with apprehension.

Of course, he wouldn't be here.

As the first guests approached the main door, she glided to meet them, inviting them to check their coats, showing them the seating plan, and suggesting they take a glass of champagne with them as they entered the function room.

As more and more guests arrived, a couple of Privates joined in greeting and directing, and she relaxed a little and backed off.

She started picking up some excitement about hurting someone important. It was rare that she'd pick up broadcasts with so much clarity, and it made her suspicious.

She started circulating among the guests, ostensibly checking they had a drink and knew where they were sitting, but really to see if she could pick up the person dreaming of harm.

And of course, she did.

It was a dreary little man, slightly balding, with a ridiculously luxurious moustache, some kind of adjutant. Presumably to the tall, distinguished man in the unmarked, black dress uniform.

Unmarked, as in no rank marked epaulettes, as if no one needed to know exactly who it was.

Minty focused on the man, and as he turned and she saw his face, she realised, of course, he didn't need rank insignia.

She'd studied under his benevolent gaze at the Academy, and pledged him her allegiance at the University every day.

It was THE Director General.

Was he aware he harboured a viper in his chest?

Not that she needed to worry. A discreet glance around the room revealed his Officers installed in strategic locations.

She glanced around for Chef, but of course, he'd be busy in the kitchens.

As the Commandant, presumably, the Director General had already seen him or would meet him after the meal.

And presumably, the DG's guys were on top of things. But even assuming his guys were on his side, they were looking for general risks. It was unlikely they'd be looking at his closest aides as threats.

There was no way she was going to let something happen to the DG on her watch. She didn't see an opportunity to approach the adjutant, let alone take off her gloves and touch his bare skin. But, for her own peace of mind, she needed to at least set a couple of her guys to watch him.

Except she'd just arrived, and didn't know any of them yet. She scanned the room, looking for someone familiar, and spotted the Private of the lights from the afternoon.

She looked at her watch and walked smartly over to him as if to issue instructions, which she was, but she hoped it would appear to relate to the function, not the DG. He stiffened to attention as she stopped in front of him.

She nodded. "Private, do you see the small man with the big moustache behind me, next to the Director General?"

"Yes Ma'am."

"Would you please choose someone else from your unit and keep an eye on him?"

"Yes Ma'am. Are we looking for something in particular?"

"I'm not sure. He's just giving off a weird vibe. Look for something odd that's not in keeping with attendance at an awards dinner."

"Yes Ma'am."

She turned to walk away, but turned her head back to look at him, "be prepared to use force Private."

"Yes Ma'am."

They walked in opposite directions.

Okay.

The DG had people looking after him, and she had people watching the adjutant. What was next?

Well, next was doing her job.

And that was getting people into the function room and seated at their tables so the event could proceed. She wanted the winners still mostly sober when they collected their awards.

Officers or not, it was going to get messy later.

She focused on rounding up the guests and encouraging them to sit at their allocated tables.

Another quick watch check and she sent a Private to signal delivery of the first course. And not long after, giving the Colonel Master of Ceremonies the go-ahead to start proceedings.

Minty stood in the background, in a corner of the room, not listening to what they said, but watching for mini-disasters in the making. Just the little things like allergic reactions, uniform failures, and cutlery drops. Just trying to keep the evening light and happy.

She saw the adjutant get up and leave the room, and pulled off her gloves as she started following him. She noticed her Private moving to intercept as well and was relieved there would be someone to assist.

She caught up with him as he left the room, and breaking protocol, grabbed his hand.

He tried to pull it free as he turned to confront her, but she kept hold of it as long as she could, asking "is everything okay Sir? Can I help you with something?"

"I'm fine," he snapped. "I'm just heading to the bathroom."

But she already knew he was trying to leave the cave because there was a bomb in a locker in the cloakroom.

It was set to go off in thirty minutes.

And if she didn't do something about it, the whole place would go up.

She checked the time and took the locker tag from his pocket, hoping his power wasn't something that would interfere with her preventing the explosion.

"Private, please secure the adjutant in the brig, and ask Chef to join me in the cloakroom immediately."

"Ma'am." He and his colleague dragged the struggling adjutant away down a side corridor where he wouldn't disturb the proceedings.

She thought she remembered seeing someone from the Bomb Squad on the guest list and double-checked the seating plan. There he was, Major Matthews, a nominee in the Outstanding Bravery category.

Apt.

She ducked inside and asked him to step outside for a moment.

He obliged. She closed the function room doors behind him, and picking up the relevant key, led him to the locker.

"Major, there's a bomb in here, and it's set to go off in about twenty-five minutes.

"As the bomber didn't place it himself, I'm pretty sure it's safe to open the locker door.

"Would you please examine it and tell me if you can defuse it in time, or if I need to evacuate the caves?"

He nodded, took the key, and opened the door.

She took a couple of steps back and bumped into Chef.

"Commandant," she started, but he waved her away.

"I've been here long enough to get the gist of it."

They waited as Major Matthews hummed to himself and delicately probed the device.

"I can disable it, but I'll need some sticks, clamps, pliers, a small Phillips screwdriver, and snips."

The Private had returned unnoticed, "Sir, I've been studying for my disposals certificate and have an Explosive Ordinance Kit Level 2 as well as a bomb suit if you'd like to use it?"

"Thanks son, run along and grab it quickly."

He turned to Minty and Chef, "It's a fairly amateur attempt, and I believe I can disable it before it goes off. Should only take five minutes or so once I've got the gear."

Minty looked at her watch, "there's twenty minutes remaining, is that enough of a margin?"

He frowned and looked up at the ceiling, "probably."

She looked at Chef, "What do you think Sir, evacuate or not?"

The Private slid the last few metres with his kit, and the Major plucked the suit from his hands and was pulling it on as the Private hit the wall.

Chef looked back at her and then his watch, "let's give it five minutes. If he's willing, Private Smith can assist the Major, and we'll see how they get on."

"Yes Sir!" said Smith

Simultaneously the Major said, "capital."

They got to work immediately. The Major called for tools as he needed them, and the Private handed them over, repeating the tools' name.

It seemed like an eternity, but in fact, it was only six minutes later the Major pulled off the hood and said "done."

They greeted the good news with a collective sigh.

"I'm guessing you don't have a bomb containment chamber?"

They shook their heads at him.

"A large pressure cooker with a couple of tea towels will do until the Squad can send someone to collect it. If you have a spare Dangerous Goods cage, we can leave it in there."

"Thank you Major," said Chef, "I'll send a private back with the cooker and tea towels, and he can show you where the cages are."

And a very little time later, the bomb was secured, the area cleaned and tidied, and it was almost as if nothing had happened.

Minty escorted the Major back to his table and had a brandy sent over to him.

She attempted to dismiss the Private, but he refused to end his shift early, so she sent him back to the function room, and arranged for a brandy sent to his quarters.

Needing a few precious moments of still, quiet time, she stood alone in the foyer, looking through the main doors and up the entry path, wrestling her composure into place.

Foiling an assassination attempt on her first day at a new post was undoubtedly more excitement than she'd imagined.

She wasn't sure she'd care to do that very often. If at all, ever again.

After a while, she became aware that the glass doors were reflecting someone standing next to her, hands clasped behind his back, and she turned to see Chef.

"Good job Lieutenant."

"Thank you Sir." She noticed a few flecks of glitter on his shoulder and reached out to brush them off.

He raised one eyebrow.

"If I may?"

He nodded, and she dusted them off, feeling a swirl of warm emotions toward her.

Then she remembered she'd taken her gloves off a hundred years ago and scrabbled in her pockets to find them and pull them on.

"There's someone who wants to meet you," he said quietly, "if you feel up to it?"

She stood to attention, and clicked her heels together, "of course Sir."

"Follow me."

He turned and led her down a side corridor to a small backstage room, opened a door and gestured her to enter.

And then closed the door behind her.

The Director General was alone in the room.

She stood to attention and saluted briskly.

"Lieutenant Hollister, I believe I owe you a great debt," he said.

"Not at all Sir, just doing my job."

"Nonetheless, I am grateful for your quick thinking."

"Thank you Sir."

"And I'd like to offer you a position in the Department of the Director General."

"Thank you Sir, but I don't see how I can help you there."

"You've demonstrated an unexpected use of your ability. It seems you may be more useful, gloves off, in a more protective capacity."

She wanted to know what the Director General hoped for, but his explicit use of the term "gloves off" suggested she didn't have permission to do that right now.

She'd have to use the usual means.

She looked up at him, studying his face and stance in a way that was hopefully not too calculating or suspicious. "Uh, thank you Sir. But I don't have training in that area."

"If it's something you want to pursue, I can fast-track your training."

She couldn't read anything either way, but rumour had it he'd ruthlessly assassinated his way into Office and you didn't do that by giving away anything a recent graduate could read.

He stood tall and straight, distinguished, and maybe a bit sexy.

Minty pictured him as she'd first seen him, surrounded, aside from his adjutant, by attractive young Officers whom he'd completely disregarded.

His immaculate uniform was spotlessly black, and his shoes were so shined they almost looked patent.

He seemed to sense her hesitation, "of course you'd have to blend in at times, sometimes you'd have to pose as a more intimate associate and wear civilian clothes. Like at events such as this."

For an instant, she could see herself on his arm wearing the long lime green, sparkly, swishy dress she'd imagined that afternoon, and wondered if he'd read her and planted the image there.

Then she remembered Chef's warm welcome, and the courtesy he showed his subordinates. And the sad smile he'd given as he opened the door to this room for her.

And there was the eager bomb-defusing Private. And all the other personnel who'd been so kind to her since she arrived just that morning.

Then there was the glitter. The glitter she'd decided would lead the way.

There was nothing glittery about the Director General, but there was glitter all around her here.

And on Chef's shoulder.

One sparkly dress couldn't compete against that.

The glitter said, stay.

She took a step back and saluted. "Thank you Sir, but I think I'm better off where I am. If that's all?"

He nodded. She spun on her heel and marched out of the room and down the corridor, away from him as fast as she could without running.

And as soon as she was a respectable distance around the corner, she bent over, retching, though she couldn't really say why.

Relief?

Disgust?

Terror?

The golden speckles in the floor seemed to reassure her, as did a warm hand on her back, "I take it you're staying then Lieutenant?" Chef asked.

"Yes Sir."

"That calls for a celebration. Why don't we quickly retire to my ready room, where there are plenty of witnesses to protect us?"

She stifled a snort, "thank you Sir."

He took her arm and half dragged, half carried her back in the kitchen's direction, "I think under the circumstances, you may, at the appropriate times, call me Josh."

"Thank you Sir, I mean Josh. And you may call me Minty."

"So Minty," he said as he pulled her over the threshold, "you've given everyone else a brandy. Would you like one too?"

"Technically, I'm still on duty Sir."

He glared at her for a moment.

"Technically, I'm still on duty, Josh."

"Under the circumstances, I think we can make an exception this time, but don't make it a habit," he said, winking.

He pulled a bottle of brandy and a couple of glasses from a drawer in his desk and poured them each a large one.

He handed one to her, and lifted his in a toast, "welcome to Cavern Caves Minty. I hope the rest of your posting proves less eventful than this."

She clinked her glass against his, "thank you Josh, I hope so too."

THE END

ABOUT THE AUTHOR

Alexandria Blaelock writes stories, some of them for *Ellery Queen's Mystery Magazine* and *Pulphouse Fiction Magazine.*

She's also written five selfhelp books applying business techniques to personal matters like getting dressed, cleaning house, and feeding your friends.

She lives in a forest because she enjoys birdsong, and the smell of gum leaves. When not telecommuting to parallel universes from her Melbourne based imagination, she watches K-dramas, talks to animals, and drinks Campari. At the same time. Discover more at www.alexandriablaelock.com.

IF YOU ENJOYED THIS STORY...

try the other Security Directorate stories

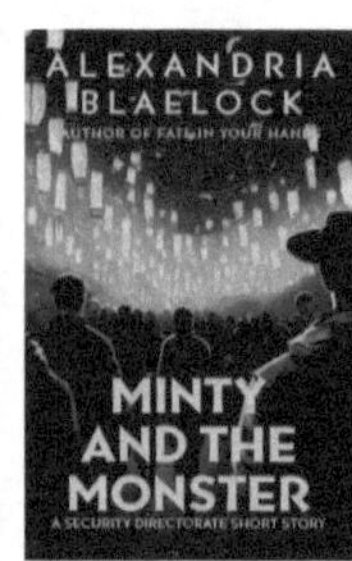

... or the collections

Why not try *The Ghost and Ms Cox*

Life interrupted

To say the letter was a surprise was an understatement. It arrived addressed to Miss Finlay Cox, which made the contents even more extraordinary.

Orphan Finn Cox inherits a cottage. Thinks it holds the key to her origins. Of course she takes a look. Who wouldn't?

But when she gets there, she gets more than she bargained for.

Is it friend, family or foe?